Dear Parent:
Your child's love of reading ....!

Every child learns to read in a different way and at his or her own speed. You can help your young reader improve and become more confident by encouraging his or her own interests and abilities. You can also guide your child's spiritual development by reading stories with biblical values and Bible stories, like I Can Read! books published by Zonderkidz. From books your child reads with you to the first books he or she reads alone, there are I Can Read! books for every stage of reading:

SHARED READING
Basic language, word repetition, and whimsical illustrations, ideal for sharing with your emergent reader.

BEGINNING READING
Short sentences, familiar words, and simple concepts for children eager to read on their own.

READING WITH HELP
Engaging stories, longer sentences, and language play for developing readers.

READING ALONE
Complex plots, challenging vocabulary, and high-interest topics for the independent reader.

ADVANCED READING
Short paragraphs, chapters, and exciting themes for the perfect bridge to chapter books.

I Can Read! books have introduced children to the joy of reading since 1957. Featuring award-winning authors and illustrators and a fabulous cast of beloved characters, I Can Read! books set the standard for beginning readers.

A lifetime of discovery begins with the magical words **"I Can Read!"**

Visit www.icanread.com for information on enriching your child's reading experience.
Visit www.zonderkidz.com for more Zonderkidz I Can Read! titles.

"The Lord does not look at the things man looks at. Man looks at the outward appearance, but the Lord looks at the heart."
—*1 Samuel 16:7*

Just Ali Cat
Copyright © 2008 by Dandi Daley Mackall
Illustrations copyright © 2008 by Janet McDonnell

Requests for information should be addressed to:
Zonderkidz, Grand Rapids, Michigan 49530

Library of Congress Cataloging-in-Publication Data

Mackall, Dandi Daley.
   Just Ali Cat / by Dandi Daley Mackall ; illustrated by Janet McDonnell.
      p. cm. -- (Ali Cat series) (I can read. Level 1)
      ISBN 978-0-310-71701-0 (softcover)
      [1. Cats--Fiction. 2. Christian life--Fiction.] I. McDonnell, Janet, 1962- ill. II. Title.
   PZ7.M1905 Juc 2008
   [E]--dc22
                                                         2008008398

Art Direction and Design: Jody Langley

Printed in China

08 09 10 • 4 3 2 1

Just Ali Cat

story by Dandi Daley Mackall

pictures by Janet McDonnell

Scritch scratch.

"What was that?" Katy asked.

Her heart went thump thump.

Ali Cat jumped onto the bed.

"It's just Ali Cat," Mom said.

Katy hugged her cat.

"Good night," Mom said.

Mom turned out the lights.

Katy went right to sleep.

The next day, Katy went to the park.

"Come swing!" Mia called to her.

Katy made her swing go high.

"Did you hear about the pet show?"
asked Mia.

"What pet show?" Katy asked.

"The Park Pet Show!" Mia said.

"The prettiest pet gets a prize.
And the smartest pet gets one too."

Katy told Mom about the pet show.

"Maybe Ali Cat can win both prizes.

She's pretty and smart," said Katy.

"Ali Cat is sweet, Katy," Mom said.

"But you did find her in the trash."

Later, Mia came over with her cat.

"Want to help me

get Fluffy ready for the pet show?"

Mia asked Katy.

"I really think she can win."

"I know who I think will win.

Wait right here!" said Katy.

Katy ran to the house.

Katy put Ali Cat inside a box.

Then she ran back to Mia and Fluffy.

"What's in the box?" Mia asked.

"The winner of the pet show!"

said Katy.

Mia peeked in. She laughed.

"It's just Ali Cat," Mia said.

Katy did not laugh.

She stared at her cat.

Ali Cat's fur stuck out funny.

Mia was right.

Ali Cat didn't look like a winner.

"Hey, Katy! Watch this!"

Dan yelled from across the street.

Dan threw a ball into the air.

His dog, Max, caught it.

"I'm getting Max ready to win

the smartest pet prize!" Dan said.

"That's it, Ali Cat!" Katy said.

"You can win for being so smart.

Lie down, Ali Cat!" Katy said.

Ali Cat sniffed a flower.

But she did not lie down.

"Okay. Sit, Ali Cat," Katy said.

Ali Cat waved her skinny tail.

But she did not sit.

"Roll over," Katy said.

"Meow," Ali Cat said.

But she did not roll over.

"Can't you do anything?"

Katy asked.

That night Mom put Katy to bed.

Katy begged Mom to tell a story.

Mom told the one about King David.

"David's brothers were big and tall.

David just took care of sheep."

"Why did God pick him?" Katy asked.

"David looked small to others.

But God looks inside," said Mom.

The next day at the pet show,

Beth's smart dog shook hands.

Jim's smart turtle bobbed to music.

Joe's talking parrot won "Smartest."

Katy wished her cat had a trick.

But Ali Cat purred in her lap,

and Katy couldn't stay sad.

One prize was left.

"The prize for the prettiest pet,"

said the man, "goes to Fluffy!"

Katy cheered for Fluffy and Mia.

Fluffy didn't like all the noise.

She scratched Mia and jumped down.

Katy ran to help.

Ali Cat licked Mia's arm.

"Thanks, Ali Cat," Mia said.

Katy hugged her cat.

She wasn't sad about not winning.

"You may not look the prettiest,

but you are prettiest on the inside.

And guess what.

God and I love insides best!"